ALIEN
INVADERS

SHE
CH

D0352406

Don't miss any of the titles
in the ALIEN INVADERS series:

ROCKHEAD: THE LIVING MOUNTAIN
INFERNOX: THE FIRESTARTER
ZILLAH: THE FANGED PREDATOR
HYDRONIX: DESTROYER OF THE DEEP
ATOMIC: THE RADIOACTIVE BOMB

ALIEN INVADERS: ATOMIC, THE RAD
A RED FOX BOOK 978

First published in Grea
an imprint of Random House Children's
A Random House Group Compan

This edition published 2011

1 3 5 7 9 10 8 6 4 2

Text and illustrations copyright © David Sinden,
Guy Macdonald and Matthew Morgan, 2011
Cover illustrations, map and gaming cards by Dynamo Design
Interior illustrations by Siku
Designed by Nikalas Catlow

The Random House Group Limited supports the Forest Stewardship
Council® (FSC®), the leading international forest certification organisation.
All our titles that are printed on Greenpeace approved FSC® certified paper
carry the FSC® logo. Our paper procurement policy can be found at
www.randomhouse.co.uk/environment

MIX
Paper from
responsible sources
FSC® C016897

Set in Century Schoolbook

Red Fox Books are published by
Random House Children's Books, 61–63 Uxbridge Road, London W5 5SA

www.**kids**at**randomhouse**.co.uk
www.**randomhouse**.co.uk

Addresses for companies within The Random House Group Limited can be
found at: www.randomhouse.co.uk/offices.htm

THE RANDOM HOUSE GROUP Limited Reg. No. 954009

A CIP catalogue record for this book is available from
the British Library.

Printed and bound in Great Britain by CPI Bookmarque,
Croydon, CR0 4TD

ALIEN INVADERS

MAX SILVER

ATOMIC
THE RADIOACTIVE BOMB

RED FOX

THE GALAXY

PLANET ZAMAN

TARN BELT

DELTA QUADRANT

GAMMA QUADRANT

PLANET ABU

PLANET OCEANIA

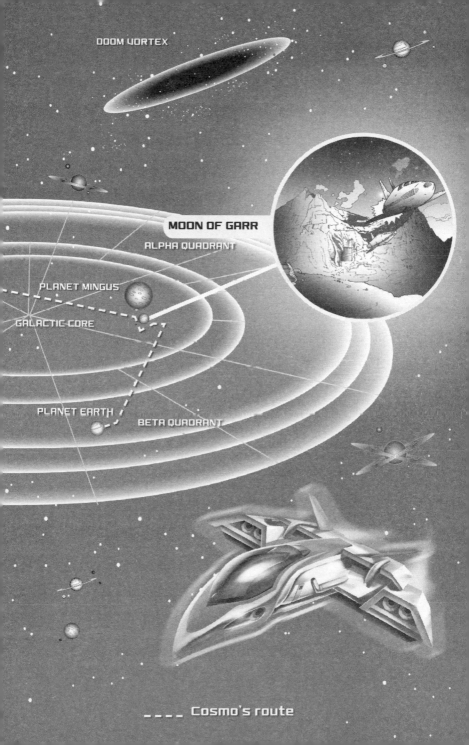

DOOM VORTEX

MOON OF GARR

ALPHA QUADRANT

PLANET MINGUS

GALACTIC CORE

PLANET EARTH

BETA QUADRANT

_ _ _ _ Cosmo's route

ATTENTION, ALL EARTHLINGS!

MY NAME IS G1 AND I AM CHIEF OF THE GALAXY'S SECURITY FORCE, G-WATCH. I BRING YOU GRAVE NEWS.

IT IS THE YEAR 2121, AND OUR PLANETS ARE UNDER ATTACK FROM THE OUTLAW KAOS. HE IS BEAMING FIVE ALIEN INVADERS INTO THE GALAXY, COMMANDING THEM TO DESTROY IT. IF THEY SUCCEED, THIS WILL BE THE END OF US ALL.

A HERO MUST BE FOUND TO SAVE US: ONE WHO WILL VENTURE THROUGH THE TREACHEROUS REGIONS OF SPACE; ONE WITH AN UNCOMMON COURAGE WITH WHICH TO FIGHT THESE INVADERS; ONE WHO POSSESSES THE POWER OF THE UNIVERSE! THAT HERO IS AN EARTHLING BOY. HE IS OUR ONLY HOPE.

INVADER ALERT!

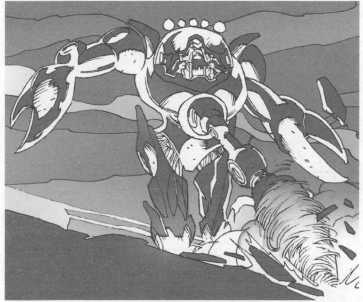

On the mining planet Abu, quarry worker
Gooka Bik powered up a drillatron
machine. Its photon battery hummed
and the machine's headlights lit up a
glowing green mist as Gooka pumped his
legs, moving its piston stilts across the
stony ground. The drillatron lurched
forward like a hulking robot, its glass-
bubble cab encasing Gooka, protecting
him from Planet Abu's toxic air.

1

Gooka was starting his shift in Abu's quarry six, mining for radonium ore – the most precious mineral in the galaxy. He guided the drillatron to the rockface, where a truck was waiting, then squeezed two triggers in its claw arms, gripping the rock with the machine's metal claws. He switched on its enormous iron drill and pressed it into the rockface. Rockdust shot out over his cab as the drill extracted large chunks of luminous green radonium ore.

Gooka lowered the drillatron's scooper, shovelling up the mineral-rich rock, then turned the machine and tipped the load onto the back of the waiting truck.

He worked for three solid Abu hours, drilling the rockface until the truck was fully loaded. "You're good to go," he radioed to the truck's android driver.

"Affirmative," came the driver's reply. Gooka wiped sweat from his hairy face as the fully-laden truck trundled down the quarry side heading for the planet's nuclear reactor. There, the radonium ore would be processed into hyperdrive cells to be used in spaceships for hyperspeed space travel.

Gooka worked for the Galactron Fuel Corporation. For half of each lunar month he would leave his family on Planet Vega and come to work on Abu. He knew the risks like all quarry workers did: exposure to the planet's toxic air could lead to radiation sickness, causing madness and even death, but the pay was high, and he was skilled at his job.

Gooka watched from his glass cab as the truck vanished into the mist, trundling onto Abu's mudflats and swamplands. He glanced to the sky, thinking of his family on Planet Vega. *Just a half-moon more and I'll be home to see you*, he thought.

A light flickered overhead and Gooka

heard a distant rumble like thunder. *Strange, no elecro-magnetic storms forecast*, he thought. The rumble grew louder, then he gasped as he saw a large object powering down from above. It slammed into the base of the quarry, and in a mighty explosion the drillatron was hurled against the rockface, its glass-bubble cab shattering.

Whoop! Whoop! Its alarm sounded, signalling that toxic air was getting in.

Gooka radioed for help: "This is Gooka Bik. Something just smashed down into quarry six. My cab's broken. Help, I'm breathing radonium gas!" His throat was tightening and he coughed.

The voice of the quarry manager Florian Dax replied from base. "Stay calm. We're coming to get you."

Still coughing, Gooka glanced back and gasped in horror. From a crater in the ground an enormous alien was rising.

I must be hallucinating, Gooka thought,
dizzy from the toxic air. He rubbed his
eyes in disbelief, but the creature was now
coming towards him! It towered taller
than the drillatron, glowing toxic green
and steaming. It roared: "I am Atomic,
and I am here on the orders of Kaos to
blow this planet up!"

CHAPTER ONE

A LONG WAY FROM EARTH

"Set a course for Planet Abu, Agent Nuri," Cosmo said.

Agent Nuri, Cosmo's blue-skinned Etrusian co-pilot, inputted the flight data into the spaceship's navigation console. "Checking available routes now," she replied.

Cosmo felt nervous but excited. He was off on the final leg of his mission for the galactic security force G-Watch, flying the

Dragster 7000 spaceship away from Planet Oceania towards the galaxy's Outer Rim.

"Done," Nuri said. She tapped the spacescreen, activating its star plotter, and words lit up on its glass:

```
DESTINATION: PLANET ABU
STAR SYSTEM: OUTER RIM
ROUTE: HYPERWAY 7 FROM SIRIUS
DISTANCE: 1.7 BILLION MILES
```

Cosmo turned the Dragster towards Sirius, a red star marked on the spacescreen. He powered the Dragster at eleven vectrons, and the cockpit filled with red starlight.

Brain-E, the ship's brainbot, bleeped from the control desk. "Steer clear of its solar flares, Master."

Cosmo had only ever seen Sirius through a telescope before – from Earth. Up close now, he saw massive explosions erupting from its surface, sending out burning solar flares. "Thanks for the warning, Brain-E," he said, nudging the steering column and giving the red star a wide berth.

"Good teamwork," Nuri smiled.

Cosmo felt glad that Nuri and Brain-E were with him. He could hardly believe he'd only known them for four Earth days, since he'd been recruited by G-Watch, the galactic security force, for a mission to save the galaxy. Cosmo had been chosen because of a power he possessed – the power of the universe, which was present in all living things but uniquely strong in Cosmo. His father, who had been an agent for G-Watch himself, had recognized the power in him when he was just a small boy.

Cosmo piloted the Dragster round Sirius then zipped between a line of space beacons onto Hyperway Seven, one of the galaxy's major space lanes. "Engaging hyperdrive now," Cosmo said, flicking a switch on the steering column. The stars turned to bright white streaks and he was thrust back into his seat as the Dragster blasted across the galaxy at hyperspeed.

Cosmo's mission was to defeat five alien invaders that had been beamed into the galaxy by the outlaw Kaos, each with orders to destroy. So far he had defeated four of them: Rockhead, the living mountain; Infernox, the firestarter; Zillah, the fanged predator; and Hydronix, destroyer of the deep. Now he was flying to Planet Abu in the galaxy's Outer Rim to face the last of the invaders: the radioactive alien Atomic.

"Prepare to exit hyperdrive on my count," Nuri said. *"Three . . . two . . . one . . . now!"*

Cosmo flicked the hyperdrive switch back and adjusted course, his ears popping as the Dragster veered off the hyperway and slowed to eight vectrons.

As the stars reappeared in the spacescreen, he stared out excitedly. *This is the furthest I've ever been from Planet Earth*, he thought. He saw docking pods where huge space-cranes were loading containers onto star freighters, and a string of floating industrial platforms stretching into the distance. "What is this place?" he asked.

Nuri tapped the spacescreen and words flashed on its glass, naming the astral objects: SUB-STATION ENERGAX ... DEPOT 5 ... GALACTRON HYPERWORKS ...

Brain-E bleeped. "The galaxy's Outer Rim is managed by the Galactron Fuel Corporation," it explained. "Hyperdrive cells for all the galaxy's spaceships are

ABU

SUB-STATION ENERGAX

manufactured in space factories here,
then taken to Planet Abu to be energized
in its radonium reactor."

*Planet Abu – that's where Kaos has
beamed Atomic*, Cosmo realized, and he
gulped nervously seeing the planet
marked on the star plotter: a remote
lump of black rock with a haze of green

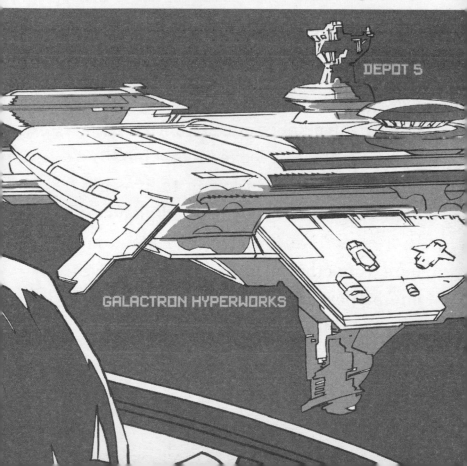

light around it. "With the invader attacking Abu, all hyperdrive capability in the galaxy could now be under threat," Cosmo said. "Hold tight. I'm taking us in."

He sped towards Abu, slicing through the planet's atmosphere, then switched to planetary mode as the Dragster roared across its sky.

Abu's sky was dark – the only light coming from a glowing green mist. Cosmo turned on the Dragster's searchlights and started to descend. Through the mist he saw the planet's surface dotted with barren hilltops. It looked like a harsh, desolate place. "Who'd want to live on a planet like this?" he wondered aloud.

"No one," Nuri replied. "Workers come here from other planets, but no one lives on Abu permanently. It's too dangerous."

A light flashed on the Dragster's external gauges:

ATMOSPHERIC WARNING: RADIOACTIVE

Brain-E bleeped. "Radonium is mined here, the most radioactive substance in the galaxy. Even the air here is toxic."

In the beam from the Dragster's searchlights, Cosmo saw mining machines working in quarries on the hillsides, and green mist swirling up from the rock.

"The mist is radonium gas," Brain-E continued. "If breathed in, radiation sickness will ensue, causing madness, then death."

Nuri checked the navigation console. "G-Watch's scanners calculated that the alien would have beamed in due east of here. Take us lower, Cosmo."

Cosmo pointed the Dragster eastwards and dived through the mist, wondering what sort of alien invader could survive in such a place. "Brain-E, what data do you have on Atomic?" he asked.

The brainbot's lights flashed. "Atomic originates from a radioactive star in the Doom Vortex, Master. He feeds on radiation and can detonate himself like a living bomb, exploding then reforming again and again."

"A radioactive living bomb!" Cosmo exclaimed, startled. Then he remembered the warning that G1, chief of G-Watch,

15

had given him when he had set off for Planet Abu: *Atomic will be the most powerful enemy you've faced.*

Cosmo gathered his courage and his spacesuit started to glow. It was G-Watch's greatest piece of technology, the Quantum Mutation Suit: a living body armour infused with particles from the beginning of the universe. Activated by the power inside Cosmo, it could transform him into fearsome alien forms.

As the Dragster cut through the swirling mist, flying close to the ground, he kept watch for the invader. He noticed a hillside quarry with a huge crater in it. "Nuri, what's that?" he asked, slowing and hovering above it.

Nuri peered down. "An impact crater!" she said. "Atomic must have beamed in *here*. Take us in to land, Cosmo."

Cosmo began his descent through the mist. But as he did, the Dragster's searchlights shone on a robot-like machine clawing frantically at the air. "That machine's going berserk. Something's wrong with it!" he said.

"It's a drillatron. Oh no, its cab's smashed!" Nuri replied.

Suddenly the machine jerked round and lunged for the Dragster, grabbing hold of it with a metal claw. *CLANG!*

"Hey, what's it doing?" Cosmo yelled.

The drillatron reached up with a second claw and clamped hold again. *CLUNK!*

"Whoa!" Cosmo struggled with the steering column as the Dragster lurched from side to side. He touched the thrusters, trying to shake the machine off, but it wasn't letting go.

"Its operator must be breathing toxic gas!" exclaimed Nuri. "He's got radiation sickness. He's going crazy!"

"Then we have to get to him, Nuri, and fix what's wrong with him before he shakes us to pieces."

CHAPTER TWO

A SHOT OF SERUM

Nuri clambered from her seat to the first-aid cabinet, trying to stay on her feet as the Dragster shook.

"What are you doing?" Cosmo asked her.

"The operator needs a shot of serum BX1 to counter the effects of the radiation sickness." From the first-aid cabinet she took out an injector gun and inserted a small phial of clear liquid into it.

The Dragster shuddered violently.

"I'll go, Nuri," Cosmo said, unbuckling his flying harness. "You take the controls."

He grabbed a plasma torch from the kit shelf then wrenched open the air-lock hatch in the floor of the cockpit.

Nuri handed him the injector gun. "You'll need oxygen too, Cosmo. You can't breathe the air out there."

Cosmo hooked the injector gun to his utility belt, then, from a pouch beside it, took a white oxygen pill. He swallowed it, pulled down his helmet's visor and lowered himself into the airlock, its hatch slamming shut behind him.

He heard Nuri over his helmet's earpiece, "Good luck!"

Cosmo opened the outer hatch and toxic mist swirled around him. He hesitated, seeing the hulking metal machine below, its claw arms clamped onto the Dragster. He summoned his courage and jumped, landing on its drill arm, gripping tightly to

its metal shaft. Just then the drill swung
upwards and struck the Dragster's hull,
sending sparks flying. Cosmo clung on and
shone his plasma torch at the drillatron's
shattered bubble cab. Its hairy-faced
operator looked wide-eyed with fear.

"Get away, monster from the sky!" the
operator yelled at the Dragster 7000.

"Stop! It's not a monster. It's my spaceship!" Cosmo called back.

But the operator pressed the drill harder, trying to bore through the Dragster's metal.

Cosmo's torch beam illuminated hydraulic cables attached to the drill, and he leaped for one, pulling it out with a hiss of steam, making the drill stop.

"Monster!" the drillatron operator called again.

The hulking machine lurched, swinging Cosmo on the cable. He let go, leaping towards the broken cab, and crashed down on the drillatron's operator. The operator was at least three times the size of Cosmo, but he looked terrified.

"I'm here to help you," Cosmo said. He quickly pressed the injector gun to the operator's arm and pulled its trigger, releasing a dose of serum BX1.

Immediately the operator calmed. His

eyes cleared, and with a look of surprise he glanced at the Dragster. "Where did that spaceship come from?" he asked.

"We're from G-Watch," Cosmo replied. "You're OK now – the toxic gas here made you a bit crazy, that's all."

"I thought it was another monster," the operator said, shakily lowering the Dragster to the ground. He switched off the drillatron's power then blinked, confused.

From the Dragster's cockpit door, Brain-E scuttled out, checking the spaceship for damage. Cosmo heard the brainbot's voice in his earpiece: "All systems intact, dents and scratches only."

Nuri stepped down and shone her torch towards Cosmo. "Well done," she called. She came running over with a spare space helmet and reached up, handing it to the operator. "Put this on," she told him.

The operator placed the helmet on his head to keep the toxic radonium gas out.

"Tell us what happened here," Nuri said.

"There was an explosion and my cab smashed. I thought I saw a monster – a freak-like alien."

"You did," Cosmo said. He shone his torch around. "Which way did it go?"

But at that moment headlights appeared round the quarry side as two open-topped buggies sped towards them. The buggies screeched to a halt and a big hairy-faced Vegaran man stepped out of the first one. He was wearing an anti-radiation helmet and a spacesuit with a Galactron Fuel Corporation badge on it. "Are you OK, Gooka?" he asked the drillatron operator.

"This man was suffering from radiation sickness," Nuri said. "He's had a dose of serum BX1, and now needs monitoring."

The big Vegaran looked down at Nuri and Cosmo. "I'm Florian Dax, Galactron quarry supervisor. Who are you?"

"We're from G-Watch," Cosmo explained. "Gooka witnessed an alien invader landing here."

The quarry supervisor chuckled. "If Gooka's inhaled toxic gas then he'll have just been hallucinating."

"But, boss, I did see it," Gooka said.

"Get him to the sick bay," the supervisor instructed two men in the other buggy. They lifted Gooka Bik down from the drillatron and put him in the back of their vehicle.

"He wasn't imagining the alien, Mr Dax," Nuri said, shining her torch into the smouldering crater. "This is an impact crater." She pointed to glowing green footprints leading from the crater down the hillside. "And something large went that way!"

The quarry supervisor looked shocked.

"We have to go after it, Mr Dax," Cosmo

added, looking down the quarry side into the mists.

"B-b-but, you can't! There are perilous mudflats and swamplands down there. Health and safety rules state that only Galactron android transporter trucks can go down there to deliver radonium ore to the nuclear reactor."

"The nuclear reactor?" Cosmo asked, concerned. He glanced at Nuri and could tell they were thinking the same thing: that Atomic might be heading to the reactor to destroy it. "Mr Dax, I'm afraid that the Galactron nuclear reactor could be in danger."

The quarry boss frowned. "But the reactor is made of solid butonium and has android security guards stationed all round it. Nothing could get in."

"Mr Dax, you don't understand what we're dealing with here," Nuri said. "This alien invader is a walking bomb."

Cosmo hopped up into the supervisor's buggy. "Can we borrow your vehicle?"

"That's company property! You'll need special authorization—"

But Cosmo had already started its engine, and Nuri and Brain-E climbed in beside him. "Thanks for the warning, Mr Dax, but we've got an alien to catch!"

And they sped off down the hillside into the mist.

CHAPTER THREE

DOWN INTO DANGER!

Cosmo pressed his foot on the accelerator, steering the open-topped buggy down the hillside through the mist, its headlights on full beam. He'd been dirt track racing with his dad on Earth and knew how to drive land vehicles on rough terrain. The buggy bumped along, with Nuri bouncing up and down in the passenger seat, and Brain-E clinging on beside her.

Cosmo and Nuri kept their visors down,

keeping out the toxic mist as they scanned the area for Atomic.

They drove out onto the crusted black mudflat, following a hard-packed trail. Cosmo saw the caterpillar tracks of a truck running along the ground, and huge glowing green footprints heading in the same direction. Even with the buggy's headlights on full beam he could only see about ten metres ahead. He kept to the hard track, trying to focus in the blinding mists, and swerved to avoid twisted gnarled trees and the half-submerged skeletons of creatures. It felt eerie, as though the invader might be lurking in wait for them along the trail.

Cosmo flinched as an insect the size of his fist splatted against his visor, leaving a smear of orange slime.

"Urgh!" Nuri said over his earpiece. "What was that?"

Cosmo wiped the slime away then

heard a strangulated cry: *Rawwwgh* . . .
Rawwwgh . . . as another weird creature
swooped through the mist over the
buggy's open top. He glanced up,
watching it fly overhead. It was a
scrawny featherless bird with three
beaky heads. "What's *that*?" he said into
his helmet's communicator.

Brain-E bleeped. "It's a toxic buzzard," the brainbot replied. "One of the few creatures that can survive in this environment: a marsh scavenger that preys on animals stuck in the mud."

It gave Cosmo the creeps, and he beeped the buggy's horn as he drove, trying to scare it away.

"Hey, look," Nuri said, shining her torch out of the side of the buggy, tracking Atomic's glowing green footprints. "Atomic's footprints are becoming more widely spaced, as if he's been running."

Cosmo saw the footprints heading to the right, and veered off the hard trail to follow them.

"Look at the truck's caterpillar tracks," Nuri said. "They're skidding and sliding all over the place."

Just then, they heard a muffled *boom!* in the distance.

"That sounded like a bomb going off!"

Cosmo said, and he jammed his foot to the floor, accelerating as fast as he could.

"Master Cosmo, do we have to go so fast?" Brain-E asked. "My circuits are jangling."

"We sure do, Brain-E," Cosmo replied, thinking that the blast might be Atomic up ahead.

It was hard to see in the mist, but about half a mile away Cosmo could make out the dim glow of a vehicle's headlights. As he sped towards them, the buggy's wheels started to skid and spray wet mud.

"Cosmo, be careful," Nuri warned. "We've veered off the trail. The mud's softer here."

The headlights were shining from a truck, but it was lying on its side, its trailer buckled and twisted. The truck's cab was mangled and its doors were blown off.

Cosmo skidded to a halt beside it.

"Atomic must be here somewhere," he
said, looking into the mist. But there was
no sign of the invader, and the only

sound he could hear was the *gloop* of bubbles rising from the mud.

"Oh no! This is sinking mud!" Nuri cried. "The truck's being swallowed up!"

Cosmo saw the truck slowly going down, being sucked into the mud. He heard a cracking sound as one of its headlights burst, then he heard an android voice call: "Unauthorized personnel alert!"

He shone his torch through the mist, and close by saw the truck's android driver. It had been flung from its cab in the explosion, and it was sinking too. "Attack on Galactron property," the android called.

"It's in trouble," Cosmo said to Nuri. He opened the buggy's door to rush to save it, but when he placed his foot on the mud he sank in right up to his thigh.

Nuri grabbed him and pulled him back in. "Cosmo, it's not safe."

Cosmo watched the android, unable to do anything to help it as the mud bubbled, swallowing it into the ground. Soon it was gone.

Brain-E bleeped. "Master Cosmo, Miss Nuri, I don't wish to alarm you, and I know we have an alien to stop, but it appears we have left the safety of the track."

Cosmo could hear glooping sounds all around the buggy. He peered over its side and saw the vehicle's wheels three-quarters submerged in the mud. It was sinking deeper with every passing second. "And now we're sinking too!"

CHAPTER FOUR

SINKING FAST

Cosmo slammed his foot down on the buggy's accelerator, but its wheels spun round and round in the mud, sinking deeper. "We have to get out of here, before we go down too."

Nuri shone her torch through the mist. The dry mud trail was more than thirty metres away.

Cosmo thought for a moment. "Perhaps if we run we could make it," he suggested.

Brain-E bleeped. "Negative, Master."

The open-topped buggy started tipping backwards and mud began seeping over the tops of its doors, into the footwells and onto the seats. Suddenly its whole rear end slid under.

"Whoa!" Cosmo said, clambering out onto its front.

Nuri and Brain-E did the same, scrambling to safety, but the mud was already seeping over their spaceboots.

Brain-E clung to Cosmo's arm, its lights flashing with panic. "Master Cosmo, by my calculations we have forty seconds until we are totally submerged. *Thirty-nine . . . thirty-eight . . . thirty-seven . . .*"

"No countdown please, Brain-E," Nuri said, starting to panic too.

Cosmo heard wings beating overhead and looked up. A flock of toxic buzzards was circling above the buggy. "Uh-oh, they've come for their dinner!"

The mud was rising up over Cosmo's legs. The buggy was sinking fast. "Nuri, I could use the Quantum Mutation Suit to transform into something to get us out of here."

"No, Cosmo. You need to save your power to fight Atomic. I've got another idea." Nuri unzipped a pouch on her utility belt and took out what looked like a small crossbow. She pressed a button on it and four sharp hooks extended from its end.

"What's that?"

"It's a grappling hook," Nuri replied. "Used for scaling buildings." She shone her torch at a gnarled tree growing alongside the dry mud trail. Then she pointed the grappling hook at it.

"Hurry," Cosmo said. He was now up to his chest in the mud, and Brain-E was clutching onto his shoulder.

Nuri pulled a trigger on the grappling hook's handle and the sharp hooks shot out, a thin metal cable stretching out behind them.

"Did you get the tree?" Cosmo asked. He couldn't see any more. Mud was coming up around his visor. Everything went pitch dark as he sank beneath the surface.

"Cosmo!" he heard in his earpiece. He felt Nuri grab hold of his arm, then heard the sound of a whirring motor. He felt himself rising, being pulled out of the mud! He rubbed his visor and saw that Nuri had a firm grasp on the

grappling hook's handle, its motor reeling in the grappling line, pulling them towards the tree. She'd done it!

Cosmo lay flat on the surface of the mud as he was dragged along. He felt his chest bump onto dry ground and got to his feet at the base of the tree. The grappling hook was stuck firm among its branches. "Nice shot, Nuri," he said, relieved.

"That was close," Brain-E added, unclasping itself from Cosmo's shoulder.

Nuri clipped the grappling hook back onto her utility belt and all three wiped themselves down.

Cosmo shone his torch along the track and saw the glowing footprints leading away ahead of them. "Atomic must have re-formed and carried on," he said. "Let's go!"

He began jogging along the track with Nuri beside him, both shining their torches, Brain-E scuttling behind.

It was even creepier travelling on foot than in the buggy. The mist thickened, and there was no engine sound to drown out the screeches of the toxic buzzards. Twisted marsh trees loomed out of the mist like monsters, and as well as that Cosmo felt the track rising slightly, making it harder going.

In his torchlight he noticed twisted trees and glowing green water to his right.

They had reached the swamplands. He paused, squinting through his visor into the mist. In the far distance, beyond the glow of the swamp, he saw the blinking lights of a large factory-style building. "Is that what I think it is?" he asked, pointing towards it.

Brain-E bleeped. "That's the Galactron nuclear reactor, Master Cosmo. Where hyperdrive cells are energized."

Cosmo saw the hard-packed trail winding around the swampy water into the mist, rutted by the tyres of Galactron trucks that had travelled to and from the reactor. It had glowing footprints stamped along it. "Well, Atomic's definitely heading to the reactor," he said.

"We've got to stop him fast," Nuri said. "If he blows the reactor, it will cause the most almighty explosion – the whole planet will go up with it!"

Cosmo had an idea. "If we cut across the swamp we can get to the reactor more quickly," he said.

"Hmm, I don't fancy swimming in that," Nuri replied, peering into the green water.

Cosmo stepped in, feeling the water rising up against his chest. "What we need is some kind of boat," he said. He shone his torch onto an old tree trunk floating among the reeds. He swam over to it and tested its buoyancy, pressing it down in the water. It bobbed, staying afloat. "We'll use this," he called. Then he broke off a branch. "And this as a paddle."

Cosmo pulled himself onto the floating log, his legs dangling either side in the cold water. "Hop aboard, you two," he said.

Nuri picked up Brain-E and stepped into the water. She clambered onto the log, sitting behind Cosmo and shining her torch across the swamp.

Brain-E perched at the front of the log to direct them. "Off we go then," the little brainbot said. "Full speed ahead to the reactor!"

Cosmo plunged the branch into the green water and swept it backwards, rowing out across the glowing swamp.

CHAPTER FIVE

PREPARING TO CELEBRATE

Meanwhile, beyond the galaxy, in a private dressing chamber on the battleship *Oblivion*, the alien outlaw Kaos was trying on a robe made of golden bones.

"Not long now before they crown me Ruler of the Galaxy," one of his heads said.

"Emperor, surely," another remarked.

"The Supreme Being," another bragged.

"The Big Cheese," a fourth said.

"El Magnifico," the fifth added.

"We will disband G-Watch and take a victory tour through the galaxy, doing as we please!"

All Kaos's five heads roared with laughter. "Oh, how marvellous!"

Just then a little purple rat squeaked from the doorway.

"What do you want, Wugrat?" Kaos asked impatiently.

Wugrat scurried to its master, squeaking several more times as if concerned.

"What's that, Wugrat? You don't think we should celebrate just yet?"

"*Eeek eek eek eeeeek.*"

"Atomic might not succeed?"

"*Eeek!!!*"

Kaos pressed his foot on the rat's tail, pinning it to the floor. "Stop fretting, you stupid little rat. Of course Atomic will succeed. He will blow Planet Abu to smithereens."

Wugrat was trying to pull its tail free.

"Anyway, Wugrat, you're meant to be
keeping an eye on Atomic's navicom
transporter signal," Kaos continued. He
kicked the little purple creature across the
floor and it scurried out through the door.

Kaos's heads looked at one another,
grinning. "Nothing can stop Atomic. He's
a radioactive bomb," one said.

"And soon the galaxy will have no
more hyperdrive cells for its spaceships,"
another laughed. "It will come to a halt!"

Kaos swished his golden robe and its
bones rattled. "G-Watch will beg for
mercy. Oh, I am brilliant."

"So am I!"

"And so am I!"

"And so am I!

"Me too!"

* * *

"We're making good progress, Master Cosmo," Brain-E said from the front of the log.

Cosmo concentrated, pulling the branch paddle through Planet Abu's swamp. It felt unnerving, his legs dangling in the glowing green water. Every now and then he spied bubbles rising to the surface.

Nuri was shining her torch. "I dread to think what creatures are lurking down there," she said over the communicator. Suddenly something splashed to their right and she swung the torch beam.

Cosmo thought he saw the tip of a tentacle, then the water rippled and went still. "What was that?" he asked.

"I don't know, but this place is creepy," Nuri replied with a shudder.

Cosmo swept the branch through the water, dragging them quickly past a clump of slimy swamp weed. He glided under the branches of a twisted tree and felt twigs scrape against his helmet.

Nuri shone her torch up ahead, and it illuminated the cab of a rusted vehicle poking up through the reeds. "Look at that," she said. "Do you think Atomic's been this way and destroyed another transporter?"

"Negative, Miss Nuri," Brain-E bleeped. The brainbot scanned its databank. "That is an old J-type transporter, last in service here over ten years ago."

Cosmo saw that the vehicle was covered in marsh slime.

"I have a record of it becoming stranded in the swamp in the year 2110, trapping eight radonium miners."

"How do you know all this, Brain-E?" Cosmo asked.

"Because G-Watch sent a rescue party to save them, led by one Agent J. Santos."

Cosmo gasped. "My father?"

"Affirmative, Master Cosmo. He saved

all eight miners from attack by a sharnippo in this very swamp. After the incident, the Galactron Fuel Corporation switched to using only android drivers."

As Cosmo paddled, he proudly thought of his dad. It had been over two years since he'd died in a space-crash, and Cosmo missed him very much. "What's a sharnippo, Brain-E?" he asked curiously.

"A carnivorous underwater tube-feeder, Master Cosmo."

At that same moment Cosmo felt something bump against his leg. "Nuri, quickly shine your light into the water."

Nuri directed her torch and all three peered down into the glowing green depths. "What's the matter, Cosmo?" she asked.

"I felt something," he replied. *I hope it wasn't a sharnippo*, he thought.

Suddenly something tugged his foot, and he lifted his boots out of the water. "There *is* something down there!"

The water stirred as something moved beneath them. A trail of bubbles rose, then a fleshy tube-like trunk shot out of the water and curled around Brain-E, pulling the brainbot in.

"A sharnippo!" Nuri cried, shining her torch.

"And it's got Brain-E!" Cosmo yelled. He handed Nuri the paddle. "Here, take this. Keep paddling as fast as you can."

He dived into the water to save the brainbot. Down he swam, through glowing green slime. He shone his torch and saw fleshy feeding tubes writhing in the water. They led to the fat blubbery body of a large squid-like creature on the bottom – the sharnippo. He saw the little brainbot being dragged down by one of its feeding tubes. Cosmo grabbed hold of it and wrenched Brain-E from its grasp. The sharnippo lashed out at him with another feeding tube, whacking his visor

hard. He kicked upwards as fast as he could and broke the surface of the water. More feeding tubes whipped up angrily. With the brainbot in one hand, he swam for his life heading for the far bank.

Nuri had paddled ashore and was reaching for him with the branch. "Grab hold of this, Cosmo."

Cosmo swam fast, the water bubbling and foaming behind him. He felt the fleshy tubes coiling round his legs. Close to the bank, he grabbed the branch and kicked as hard as he could, Nuri dragging him ashore to safety. "Nice one, Nuri," he said, grateful to be free from the grip of the sharnippo.

Brain-E scuttled from his hand. "Thank you, Master Cosmo. You saved me."

"No problem, Brain-E."

Cosmo got to his feet and shook himself dry. Having made it across the swamp, he stared through the mist towards the lights of the large reactor building. "A sharnippo is nothing compared to what we have to face," he said. "Let's go find Atomic!"

All three hurried through the reeds towards the reactor. But as Cosmo ran, he found it difficult to breathe. He felt dizzy and weak. In the mist he thought he saw a face, then another, then three more. "Here, let me help you," a hideous voice snarled in his ear. He stopped running, confused, and saw a gnarled hand reaching towards him. It was a five-headed alien, glaring at him! Cosmo blinked disbelievingly.

"Cosmo, are you OK?" he heard in his earpiece.

He blinked again, and the alien disappeared. Instead he saw Nuri standing in front of him, offering him her hand.

This is freaky, Cosmo thought. "Nuri, I think there's something wrong with me . . ."

His mind was swirling and he could feel sweat dripping down his face.

Nuri peered at his visor. "Oh no! Cosmo, your visor's got a crack in it. You're hallucinating! You're inhaling radonium gas!"

CHAPTER SIX

FACING THE ENEMY

Cosmo's mind was swimming with confusion. Brain-E was bleeping, but to Cosmo the brainbot sounded like a ticking bomb. "Brain-E's going to explode, Nuri!" he said.

Suddenly he felt a sharp prick in his neck, and through his visor he saw Nuri holding a syringe gun with Brain-E clinging to her wrist, shining a light into his eyes.

"Pupils dilating. Rapid eye movement," he heard the brainbot say. "It was definitely radiation sickness, Miss Nuri."

Cosmo could feel himself slowly coming round, his mind clearing. He felt calmer and realized that Nuri had injected serum BX1 into his bloodstream.

Brain-E shone a laser from one of its probes, sealing the tiny crack in his visor.

"What happened?" Cosmo asked, breathing steadily once more.

"You were inhaling toxic air," Brain-E said. "Hallucinating from radiation sickness."

"It was like a nightmare."

"Well, thank goodness you're OK now," Nuri said.

"My visor must have cracked when the sharnippo struck it," Cosmo said. "Thanks, you two."

"We're a team, remember. We look out for each other," Nuri told him.

Cosmo smiled. He was just getting his breath back when he heard the sound of phaser fire in the distance. It was coming from the direction of the reactor. "That sounds like the android security guards firing! Quick, they must be under attack!"

Cosmo, Nuri and Brain-E ran towards the nuclear reactor. A huge section of its perimeter fence had been ripped open.

"Hurry!"

They rushed through the huge hole, and in the reactor's concrete compound saw a mighty alien stomping through the android guards. It was twenty times their size, glowing green and bulging with muscles. It roared: "OUT OF MY WAY!"

"It's Atomic!" Cosmo said.

The android security guards were firing at the invader, but their phaser beams were bouncing off it.

"YOU CANNOT HURT ME!" Atomic roared. His body glowed brighter,

steaming like a volcano. "BUT I CAN
HURT YOU!" In a massive blast and a
flash of green light, the alien exploded
into pieces.

The force of the blast hurled Cosmo and Nuri backwards, chunks of rock and android parts showering down on them.

Cosmo sat up, dazed. Where Atomic and the android guards had stood, only debris remained. He reached for Nuri. "Are you OK?"

"I'm alive, if that's what you mean," she replied.

Brain-E bleeped beside them. "Uh-oh. So is Atomic. Look!"

Cosmo watched in fear as chunks of glowing green rock and bubbling green mucus began moving across the ground and flying through the air. They were dragging chunks of radonium ore and android body parts with them. It was as if they were being blown by a strong wind, the debris sticking together in mid-air, forming a monstrous alien body. It was Atomic re-forming. Its legs came together, then its torso, and the alien's weird body began marching across the compound, heading for the main reactor building.

He's going to blow it up, Cosmo thought desperately. "Nuri, Brain-E, stay back," he whispered into his helmet's mic.

"Cosmo, what are you doing?" Nuri asked over his earpiece.

"It's time to use the Quantum Mutation Suit."

He raced through the broken androids in pursuit of the alien. "Hey, freakshow – get away from there!" he called out.

Atomic turned to face Cosmo and roared: "Who dares challenge me?"

"Cosmo Santos, G-Watch agent! And I've got something to show you!" Cosmo felt his power welling inside him and his Quantum Mutation Suit glowed. "SCAN," he said into the helmet's sensor. Digital images of aliens flashed on his visor as the Quantum Mutation Suit searched through its databank: an

arrow-winged vultron . . . a fire-horned bullzoth . . . a warp-speed panthax . . .

Which alien is powerful enough to withstand an explosion? he wondered. He assessed their heights, weights and features, then focused on an image of a large armour-plated alien:

ALIEN: CHOD
SPECIES: AARDGARK
ORIGIN: PLANET RUDRON
HEIGHT: 13 METRES
WEIGHT: 5 TONNES
FEATURE: METAL EXOSKELETON

An aardgark with a metal exoskeleton! Perfect! Cosmo thought. "MUTATE!"

CHAPTER SEVEN

DANGER: HIGH EXPLOSIVE

Cosmo felt his body tingle as the Quantum Mutation Suit fused with his flesh. It began re-forming his molecular structure, making him grow larger with big bulging muscles. His skin hardened into thick metal scales that shone like armour, covering him from head to feet. He was Chod, the aardgark, and he felt powerful like a machine. "I am Chod. And I am here to stop you!"

Cosmo charged at Atomic, dipping his shoulder and going into a forward roll. He spun like a huge demolition ball across the yard and smashed into the invader, sending him sprawling on the ground. Cosmo rose to his feet between Atomic and the reactor. "You will not pass me!" he said.

"Out of the way, metal-head, or be blown up too!" Atomic replied.

Cosmo pulled back his fist and smashed it into Atomic's stomach, shattering the alien's belly. Then he whacked the invader's jaw, sending chunks of green rock flying.

But Atomic just laughed. "Haahhaahaa! You can't destroy me!" He began glowing more brightly, steam jetting from his body. Then, in a burst of green light, he exploded.

Cosmo braced himself, shielding the reactor, as chunks of rock clattered against

his metal exoskeleton: as Chod, he was
blast-proof. All around him the ground
was strewn with debris: radonium ore,
android body parts and hideous green
gunk from the invader. But the reactor
was still standing, Chod's body having
protected it from the blast.

"Are you all right, Cosmo?" Nuri called. She came running towards him over fallen guards, with Brain-E attached to her wrist.

"RESET!" Cosmo said. He felt his body tingling as he turned back into his boy self. "Yes, but this invader's completely insane!"

"Uh oh, he's re-forming again!" Brain-E said, pointing a metal leg at bits of rock and debris stirring in the yard. They were flying up from the ground towards a second building with pipes coming off it connected to the reactor. Atomic was re-forming on the building's rooftop.

"That's the cooling tower that pumps water into the reactor to stop it overheating," Brain-E said. "If he blows it up, the reactor will go into meltdown. It'll explode from the inside!"

Cosmo saw the invader re-forming, first his legs, then his belly . . .

"Nuri, Brain-E, see if there's a way to

shut the reactor down. I'll deal with Atomic."

I've got to get him off that building, Cosmo thought. He spoke into his helmet's sensor: "SCAN." The Quantum Mutation Suit glowed as images of aliens appeared on its visor's digital display: a gore-toothed rhinox . . . a sabre-fisted tae-quan . . . an electric storm-shark . . . Cosmo saw a huge eagle-like alien with sharp talons.

ALIEN: PADLON
SPECIES: EAGLART
ORIGIN: PLANET EGRA
HEIGHT: 3 METRES
WEIGHT: 2 TONNES
SPECIAL FEATURES: RAZOR-SHARP TALONS

With talons I could grab that invader. "MUTATE!" he yelled.

Cosmo felt his body tingling again. He grew bigger, and feathers sprouted from his skin. His feet lengthened and hardened into huge talons, and large eaglart wings emerged from his back. He

beat them and took off, soaring high into the mist. As Paolon, he was swift. He flew towards the cooling-tower roof where Atomic was re-forming. The invader's legs and body had already taken shape, and debris was flying towards them, forming his arms and hands.

Cosmo reached out with his talons trying to grab the invader, but Atomic's massive fist swiped at him. Cosmo ducked and swooped, avoiding it. He gripped hold of Atomic's half-formed body and tried to lift him from the cooling

tower, but the invader was heavy, and
getting heavier all the time, his body parts
gathering as Paolon's talons pulled. With
all his eaglart strength, Cosmo beat his
wings, and the alien began rising a little.

Atomic's head flew back on and

roared: "YOU CANNOT STOP ME!"
He glowed green, steam pouring from
his body, and in a blinding flash of light
the invader exploded.

Cosmo was hurled through the air by
the blast, and crashed down into the yard.
He lay dazed, his wings crumpled and
his feathers singed. Aching with pain,
Paolon's molecular pattern was breaking

up. "RESET," Cosmo said, and his broken eaglart body transformed back into a boy.

He glanced across the compound to the cooling tower. The explosion had blown its pipes apart and water was pouring from them. A siren sounded from the main reactor: *Nark! Nark! Nark!*

The reactor was about to overheat!

CHAPTER EIGHT

MELTDOWN

Cosmo heard Nuri's voice over his earpiece. "Cosmo, are you OK?"

He looked for her among the destruction, and saw her standing by an open metal doorway at the side of the reactor building. "I'm OK," he replied into his mic. "Did you find a way to shut down the reactor?"

"Brain-E's working on it now," Nuri told him.

Cosmo got to his feet and saw chunks

of debris and bubbling green mucus stirring on the ground. He raced to the main reactor building and dashed inside with Nuri, slamming the door shut behind them. "How did you get in?" he asked.

"Brain-E picked the digital lock."

Cosmo saw the brainbot inside a gleaming white room, scuttling along a huge control desk with rows of computers. The warning siren was blaring and lights were flashing alerts.

"Brain-E, the cooling tower is down," Cosmo said. "You have to stop the reactor or it will blow."

The brainbot bleeped, extending a probe arm into a control panel. "I'm trying to access the emergency shutdown protocol, but it's security protected and the code's four-hundred digits long."

Behind a toughened-glass window Cosmo could see the reactor's core: a huge lump of hot radonium, radiating

bright green light. It was glowing
dangerously, heating up.

Brain-E scuttled along the bank of
computers. "If I can crack the code, then
the emergency shutdown will release
supercooled hydrogen into the reactor."

"Supercooled hydrogen?"

"It's the coldest substance in the

galaxy," Brain-E explained. "It will instantly cool the reactor's core."

But as the brainbot tried to hack into the reactor's main computer, chunks of green rock and globs of mucus started flying in through a purifying air vent on the wall and binding together inside the control room. Atomic had found a way into the building! The alien's arm started re-forming, and more rocks flew together to make his torso.

"Nuri, we can't let Atomic reform!" Cosmo yelled.

They began snatching up the chunks of rock and throwing them to opposite sides of the room, trying to keep Atomic in pieces. But it was no use; the rocks were pulling together faster than Cosmo and Nuri could keep them apart.

Brain-E bleeped. "I'm in! Shutdown procedure commencing." The brainbot scuttled along the computer keypad,

pressing a sequence of buttons.

Atomic's head flew back on, his mad eyes blazing. "Shutdown procedure aborted!" he roared, his body glowing, steam hissing from it.

Cosmo threw himself at Nuri to protect her as Atomic exploded in a burst of green light. He felt an intense heat on his back, then a warning blared over loudspeakers, "*ALL PERSONNEL EVACUATE . . . ALL PERSONEL EVACUATE . . .*"

He picked himself up. "Are you OK, Nuri?"

"Thanks to you I am, Cosmo," she replied.

He saw Brain-E on the floor and the computers blown to pieces.

"I did my best, Master," Brain-E said weakly. "But I'm afraid there's no way of stopping the reactor now."

Cosmo glanced at the toughened-glass window. It was now shattered. In the reactor's core, the huge chunk of radonium was glowing brighter and sparking. He could feel its heat. It was about to blow. *It's down to me now*, he thought. He leaped through the broken window, shielding his eyes from the bright light and the intense heat.

"SCAN," he said into the Quantum Mutation Suit's voice sensor. On the visor of his helmet, images of aliens began forming. *I need something as cold as supercooled hydrogen*, he thought. He stopped on an image of an icy blue alien.

ALIEN: FREEZOTH
SPECIES: ICE-SERPENT
ORIGIN: PERFIDIAN
HEIGHT: 12 METRES
WEIGHT: 1 TONNE
FEATURE: FREEZING BREATH OF -273.15 DEGREES C

Freezoth it is! "MUTATE!"

Cosmo felt a tingling sensation again as the molecules in his body re-formed into the alien, Freezoth. His temperature was dropping, and his legs fused into a serpent's tail. Wings sprouted from his sides and his flesh transformed into shimmering ice crystals. He breathed out and frost formed in the air.

As Freezoth, Cosmo beat his wings, rising in front of the core. He took a deep breath, then exhaled. A gale of freezing cold air blasted against the reactor's core. Almost instantly, the temperature of the reactor began to cool. The radonium core stopped glowing

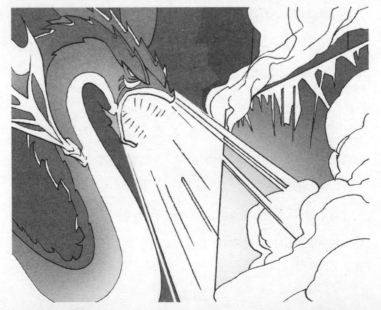

and turned to a lump of blue ice.

Cosmo collapsed, breathless, on the floor. *I've done it!* he thought. *I've stopped the reactor!*

"RESET," he gasped, and his body changed back into his boy self.

"You may have saved the reactor, Earthboy, but you can't save your friends!"

Cosmo spun round and saw Atomic re-forming in the control room. He had Nuri and Brain-E in his grasp.

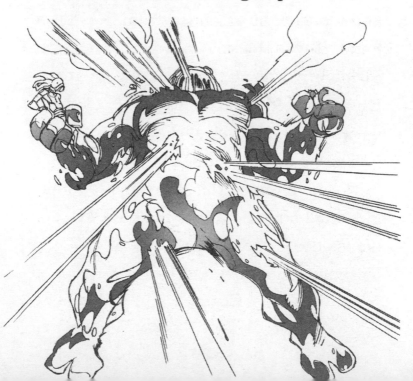

"Say goodbye to them!" the invader roared, his body glowing brightly about to explode.

Cosmo stepped towards him. "Leave them alone!"

"Cosmo, save yourself," Nuri called. "Get out of here! He's going to blow!"

Cosmo felt so angry seeing his friends in danger that his power welled up inside him, stronger than ever. The Quantum Mutation Suit glowed brightly, and blue and white light extended from his gloved hand. It was the power sword, the power inside him taking the form of a weapon. He pointed it towards Atomic. "Let them go or face the power of the universe!"

The invader roared: "Ha! Too la—"

Cosmo plunged the sword into Atomic's glowing body and a look of shock swept across the invader's face. The alien's grip loosened, and Nuri and Brain-E dropped from his hands. Cosmo could feel every

molecule of his body battling with
Atomic's radioactive force. The power
of the universe inside him was winning:
the alien's glow started fading, his green
flesh turning darker. It was hissing.

All at once Atomic shrieked: 'Noooooo!"
And he evaporated in a burst of steam.

CHAPTER NINE

MISSION ACCOMPLISHED

Cosmo collapsed to his knees, exhausted. *I've done it! I've defeated Atomic!*

He saw Nuri and Brain-E beside him, blackened with soot from the explosion. Nuri was smiling. "Mission complete," she said. "Atomic's gone!"

Brain-E was hobbling across the wrecked computers. "Well done, Master Cosmo! Planet Abu is safe!"

Cosmo looked around at the mangled

control room. "It's going to take a little while to repair this place and get the reactor fired up again. Maybe we should get out of here before the Galactron Fuel Corporation ask us to help clean up!"

Nuri laughed and helped Cosmo to his feet. They headed outside, where the remaining android security guards were picking over the debris.

"Come on, let's get back to the Dragster," Cosmo said.

Brain-E bleeped. "Oh, please don't tell me we have to go back through that swamp."

On the far side of the reactor compound, Cosmo spotted a Galactron shuttleship used for transporting workers. "This way, Brain-E," he said, heading towards it. "We'll borrow this ship and be there in no time."

**

Meanwhile, beyond the galaxy in the control bay of the battleship *Oblivion*, a squeaking could be heard. Wugrat was peering at a blank monitor. It tapped the screen with its claws. It tapped it again. Then it squeaked even louder.

Kaos's five heads peered in through the doorway. "What's the matter Wugrat?"

Wugrat glanced round at the alien

outlaw, quivering. It squeaked again and Kaos marched over.

"What do you mean you 'lost Atomic's navicom signal'?" Kaos picked the wugrat up by its tail. "We can't have lost the signal. That would mean Atomic's—"

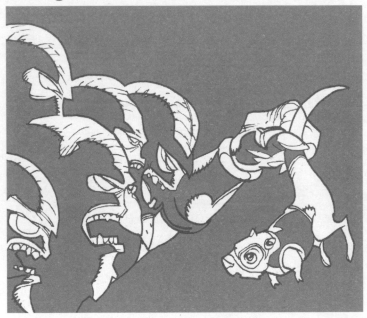

Kaos's five heads looked at one another, each fuming with anger. "He's destroyed!" they all said at once.

Kaos flung Wugrat across the room. "Blasted G-Watch!" one head roared.

"They've beaten Atomic," another said.

"It's not possible!"

"This is an outrage!"

"What now? The invaders from the Doom Vortex are defeated."

Kaos paced to and fro, fuming with anger. "This cannot be allowed to happen. We shall not be beaten! Not ever!"

***

When Cosmo, Nuri and Brain-E finally got back to the Dragster they found a note wedged onto its spacescreen: *Unauthorized parking. Penalty fee waived due to exceptional circumstances. Thank you, from Florian Dax.*

Cosmo smiled to himself then stepped aboard to radio G-Watch headquarters with the good news. He pressed a button on the communications console and its monitor flickered, showing the face of G1.

"Mission accomplished, G1," Cosmo

said. "Atomic won't be troubling the galaxy any more."

The silver-eyed Chief of G-Watch smiled. "Congratulations, Cosmo," he said. "When you are ready, return to base. Your mission is complete."

"We'll be on our way soon, G1," Nuri said. "Brain-E's just checking the ship for takeoff."

The brainbot's probe arm was inserted into the control desk and its lights were flashing. "All systems go," it said. "See you soon, G1."

The monitor's screen flickered and the transmission ended.

Cosmo fastened his harness for takeoff, then started the Dragster's thrusters. He turned to Nuri, relieved. "The galaxy is saved, Nuri. The Galactron Fuel Corporation can continue its work here on Planet Abu, and there will be hyperdrive cells for all the galaxy's spaceships."

He pulled back the throttle and the thrusters roared as the Dragster 7000 blasted up through the mist. "Set a course for Garr. We're going back to HQ."

CHAPTER
TEN

A HOMECOMING SURPRISE

Cosmo could hardly believe his mission was over. It had begun only five Earth days ago, and now he was about to land back on the moon of Garr, where he'd been recruited as a G-Watch agent. Having travelled across the galaxy at hyperspeed, the Dragster 7000 veered round the liquid-metal Planet Mingus, then down into the crimson sky of Garr.

Cosmo flew along a canyon towards

G-Watch's secret mountain headquarters, recollecting the first time he'd been here. So much had happened since: the five alien invaders from the Doom Vortex had all been defeated: Rockhead, the living mountain; Infernox, the firestarter; Zillah, the fanged predator; Hydronix, destroyer of the deep; and now Atomic, the radioactive bomb. The galaxy was safe again.

"Nuri, what will I do now that my mission is over?" he asked.

"I guess that depends on you. Do you want to go back to Earth?" she replied.

Cosmo missed his mum, and he'd like to see his friends' faces at school when he returned to tell them of his adventures, but part of him didn't want to leave G-Watch – he was an agent now, just like his father had been, and he liked it. *Besides, Kaos is still out there somewhere*, he thought to himself.

He flew the Dragster in through the side of G-Watch's mountain headquarters to the spacefleet bay where G-Watch scientists and mechanics were at work. He touched down, attaching his spaceship to the bay's docking magnets, then switched off its power. He unfastened his flying harness and stepped out, followed by Nuri.

The scientists and mechanics saluted him. He saluted back, feeling proud.

Brain-E stayed in the Dragster's cockpit as G-Watch mechanics set to work to service the spaceship after all its adventures. Cosmo and Nuri jumped onto hoverboards and headed up to the surveillance room to find G1.

"Welcome," G1 said as they entered. He was at the control desk in front of the video wall, observing satellite images from across the galaxy. "The galaxy is at peace again, thanks to you both."

He turned to Cosmo, his silver eyes shining. "You have shown bravery in the face of extreme danger, Agent Santos, and saved the galaxy from certain destruction. For that, G-Watch awards you its highest rank: G-Watch Agent Supreme."

Cosmo gasped. "Agent Supreme! Me?"

G1 nodded.

"I am honoured," Cosmo replied.

"You earned it, Cosmo," Nuri told him.

Operatives and agents working at other desks in the surveillance room all stood and cheered.

"Oh, do shut up!" a shrill voice called out. On the video wall, an image of a five-headed alien appeared, scowling furiously.

Nuri stared. "It's Kaos!"

Cosmo stood there, stunned, seeing the alien slowly drift outwards, leaving the video image and entering the room! It was floating towards him. "W-what's—"

"It's a hologram!" Nuri said.

"You're not welcome here, Kaos," G1 said. "Not as a hologram, not in the flesh – not even as a bad smell."

Kaos's heads looked angry. The hologram hovered in front of Cosmo, its five faces glaring at him. "So it was *you* who ruined my plans. A mere Earthling, I see."

"My name is Cosmo Santos, and I'm not afraid of you," Cosmo replied.

Kaos peered down at him. "Another Santos, eh?" His ten holographic eyes

stared into Cosmo's. "I knew your father, James Santos."

Cosmo froze, startled by the mention of his father's name.

G1 stepped between Cosmo and the hologram. "Kaos, I order you to leave," he said.

Kaos's heads glared at G1. "G-Watch may have defeated the invaders from the Doom Vortex, but I am not finished yet." He pointed to the video wall. "Those five brutes were just the beginning. Now prepare to meet your new worst nightmares."

On the video wall, the screens flickered and a small furry creature appeared licking its whiskers.

Kaos's five heads frowned. "Wugrat, what are you doing? You're supposed to have them ready."

The wugrat squeaked, then reached out, moving the camera to reveal five enormous aliens in the cargo hold of the battleship *Oblivion*. They were weird, hideous creatures, half-alien and half-robot.

"Behold, the android outcasts of the Wrecking Zone," Kaos said. "Did you really think I'd give up? Each will be programmed to carry out my orders, and this time there will be no mistakes. This time G-Watch will stand no chance. In precisely one Garr hour, I shall launch a new attack. The galaxy shall be mine! Mine! Mine! Mine! Mine!"

With Kaos's voices echoing around the room, the hologram drifted backwards to the video wall, then the screen flickered and went blank.

Cosmo heard G-Watch agents muttering to one another. "G1, what are we going to do now?" he asked.

G1 frowned. "It looks like you have a new mission, Cosmo. If you'll accept it, that is."

"You bet!" Cosmo said. "I'll fight those android invaders and stop Kaos once and for all!"

"I'll come too!" Nuri said.

"And me!" Brain-E added.

"OK, check all interstellar scanners," G1 commanded the agents at the surveillance computers. "Find where those invaders are headed."

Cosmo looked up at G1. "G1, there's just one thing: could you get a message to my mother on Earth to tell her I'm safe, but that I may not be back for a while?"

"Right away," G1 replied.

Cosmo saluted. "Thank you."

Then, as G1 commanded proceedings, Cosmo left with Nuri, heading back to the Dragster. He was thinking about what Kaos had said to him. "Nuri, what did Kaos mean, he knew my father?" he asked.

Nuri turned to him with a look of concern. "It's a long story, Cosmo. I'll tell you on the way."

Join Cosmo on his next mission to defeat the **ALIEN INVADERS** of the

WRECKING ZONE

Far beyond our galaxy is a
deep-space dumping ground for
waste technologies known as
THE WRECKING ZONE.

Over thousands of years, in its
wastelands, mutant aliens have evolved –
half-living, half-machine! And now they are
set to invade . . .

Are you ready to fight?

ALIEN INVADERS books six to ten are
out in early 2012. For the latest
updates on the invasion go to
www.**ALIENINVADERS**.co.uk

NOW IT'S YOUR TURN TO DO BATTLE!

Have you collected the
ALIEN INVADERS gaming cards?

In the first five books you'll find these twenty gaming cards plus two bonus cards that you can download from the **ALIEN INVADERS** website

ROCKHEAD

Rockhead the living mountain comes from the barren planet of Cojon, and battles Cosmo at G-Watch headquarters.

INTELLIGENCE	22
SPEED	65
STRENGTH	100
FREAK FACTOR	55
POWER OF THE UNIVERSE	60

HAMMERFIST

Hammerfist is an Ogron from Planet Ajax, with an iron punch that can knock out his opponents.

INTELLIGENCE	30
SPEED	31
STRENGTH	88
FREAK FACTOR	60
POWER OF THE UNIVERSE	52

MUCOSA

Mucosa, a slugoid from Planet Agar, has sliming glands all over his body, enabling him to trap enemies with his sticky slime.

INTELLIGENCE	54
SPEED	8
STRENGTH	15
FREAK FACTOR	95
POWER OF THE UNIVERSE	40

COSMO

Cosmo, an Earthling boy, possesses the Power of the Universe, and can use the Quantum Mutation Suit to transform into any alien form.

INTELLIGENCE	95
SPEED	60
STRENGTH	60
FREAK FACTOR	70
POWER OF THE UNIVERSE	100

INFERNOX

Infernox comes from Bedzin-5, an ever-expanding sun in the Boom Vortex, and has the ability to hurl fireballs and breathe fire.

INTELLIGENCE	58
SPEED	65
STRENGTH	75
FREAK FACTOR	77
POWER OF THE UNIVERSE	65

KAOS

Kaos is a five-headed alien outlaw with one goal: to take control of the galaxy.

INTELLIGENCE	98
SPEED	22
STRENGTH	32
FREAK FACTOR	85
POWER OF THE UNIVERSE	40

MAGMUS

A lava bear from Planet Vulcana, Magmus has explosive strength and heat-resistant armour plating to protect himself from attack.

INTELLIGENCE	55
SPEED	70
STRENGTH	70
FREAK FACTOR	50
POWER OF THE UNIVERSE	50

DECAGORG

Decagorg is a mega-squid from Planet Seamar. He is able to swim fast underwater and is armed with six grappling tentacles.

INTELLIGENCE	55
SPEED	80
STRENGTH	60
FREAK FACTOR	40
POWER OF THE UNIVERSE	55

www.**ALIENINVADERS**.co.uk

ZILLAH

Zillah is a female scavenger from the Doom Vortex who feeds on space wreckage in the vortex's treacherous storm zones.

INTELLIGENCE	75
SPEED	70
STRENGTH	75
FREAK FACTOR	85
POWER OF THE UNIVERSE	70

☐

NURI

Nuri, a blue-skinned Etrusian girl, is a G-Watch agent and co-pilot to Cosmo on his missions to defeat the alien invaders.

INTELLIGENCE	85
SPEED	55
STRENGTH	55
FREAK FACTOR	59
POWER OF THE UNIVERSE	65

☐

LASARG

An Argonite from Planet Kavo, Lasarg has laser-eyes than he can use as devastating weapons.

INTELLIGENCE	70
SPEED	58
STRENGTH	48
FREAK FACTOR	75
POWER OF THE UNIVERSE	70

☐

LUCONA

A star fly from the Jittasian Star Nursery, Lucona is small but very powerful, and glows with the brightness of a brand-new star.

INTELLIGENCE	10
SPEED	75
STRENGTH	5
FREAK FACTOR	85
POWER OF THE UNIVERSE	85

☐

HYDRONIX

Hydronix is an underwater alien from the Whirlpool of Dahl, with eight tentacles strong enough to crush rock.

INTELLIGENCE	65
SPEED	70
STRENGTH	92
FREAK FACTOR	45
POWER OF THE UNIVERSE	75

☐

BRAIN-E

Brain-E, who accompanies Cosmo on his missions, is a G-Watch brainbot, programmed with information from across the galaxy.

INTELLIGENCE	95
SPEED	30
STRENGTH	18
FREAK FACTOR	20
POWER OF THE UNIVERSE	15

☐

GAURON

Gauron is a gigantacrab from Planet Crux, armed with a thick shell and massive pincers strong enough to cut through metal.

INTELLIGENCE	52
SPEED	40
STRENGTH	65
FREAK FACTOR	58
POWER OF THE UNIVERSE	43

☐

ELECTRAX

A pulse serpent from Planet Reel, Electrax is able to deliver powerful electric shocks when attacked.

INTELLIGENCE	28
SPEED	75
STRENGTH	57
FREAK FACTOR	62
POWER OF THE UNIVERSE	50

☐

ATOMIC

Atomic comes from a radioactive star in the heart of the Doom Vortex. He can detonate himself and reform, like a living bomb.

INTELLIGENCE	55
SPEED	40
STRENGTH	95
FREAK FACTOR	100
POWER OF THE UNIVERSE	70

☐

G1

G1, the silver-eyed chief of G-Watch, is from the ancient planet of Oracion, and protects the galaxy from invasion.

INTELLIGENCE	100
SPEED	40
STRENGTH	57
FREAK FACTOR	59
POWER OF THE UNIVERSE	95

☐

FREEZOTH

An ice-serpent from Planet Perfidian, Freezoth resembles a dragon with cold-resistant scales and a freezing breath of -273.25°C.

INTELLIGENCE	55
SPEED	42
STRENGTH	40
FREAK FACTOR	65
POWER OF THE UNIVERSE	51

☐

CHOD

Chod is an Bardgark from Planet Rudron. He has a metal exoskeleton that defends him against even the most powerful electric explosions.

INTELLIGENCE	42
SPEED	75
STRENGTH	75
FREAK FACTOR	55
POWER OF THE UNIVERSE	50

☐

NOW YOU CAN PLAY ALIEN INVADERS TOO . . .

HOW TO PLAY
ALIEN INVADERS

Challenge a friend to do battle.

Shuffle the cards and deal them equally between you.

Look at your top card and choose a category.

If the value for that category is higher than your opponent's, you win their card.

If the value is lower, they win your card and pick the next category.

If the values are the same, then put the cards in a pile and play another round: the winner takes all the cards in the pile.

The champion is the first to win all the cards.

Pick a category

How powerful are you?

G1, the silver-eyed chief of G-Watch, is from the ancient planet of Oraclon, and protects the galaxy from invasion.

INTELLIGENCE   100
SPEED   40
STRENGTH   57
FREAK FACTOR   59
POWER OF THE UNIVERSE 95

GOOD LUCK!
THE POWER OF THE UNIVERSE IS IN YOU!

ABOUT THE AUTHOR

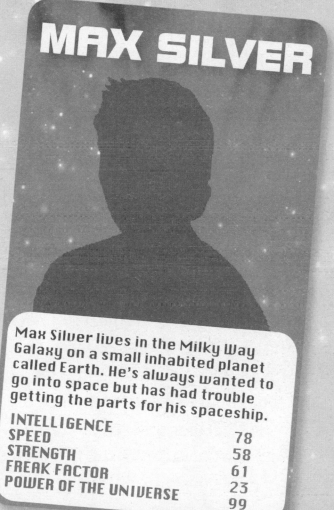

MAX SILVER

Max Silver lives in the Milky Way Galaxy on a small inhabited planet called Earth. He's always wanted to go into space but has had trouble getting the parts for his spaceship.

INTELLIGENCE	
SPEED	78
STRENGTH	58
FREAK FACTOR	61
POWER OF THE UNIVERSE	23
	99

THE TER-MOO-NATORS
by Steve Cole

IT'S 'UDDER' MADNESS!

Genius cow Professor McMoo and his trusty sidekicks, Pat and Bo, are the star agents of the C.I.A. – short for COWS IN ACTION! They travel through time, fighting evil bulls from the future and keeping history on the right track . . .

When Professor McMoo invents a brilliant TIME MACHINE, he and his friends are soon attacked by a terrifying TER-MOO-NATOR – a deadly robo-cow who wants to mess with the past and change the future! And that's only the start of an incredible ADVENTURE that takes McMoo, Pat and Bo from a cow paradise in the future to the SCARY dungeons of King Henry VIII . . .

It's time for action. COWS IN ACTION

ISBN: 978 1 862 30189 4

Stand together . . . Battle as one!
Meet THE ARMOURON – elite warriors who banded
together centuries ago to fight for justice and freedom.
But now, it's time for a new generation of the Armouron . . .
Time to buckle on the armour and take up the challenge!
Don't miss this exciting new series!

Have you got what it takes to
be the next Armouron Knight?
Take the Armouron challenge at
www.armouronbooks.co.uk

For the latest news go to
www.ALIENINVADERS.co.uk

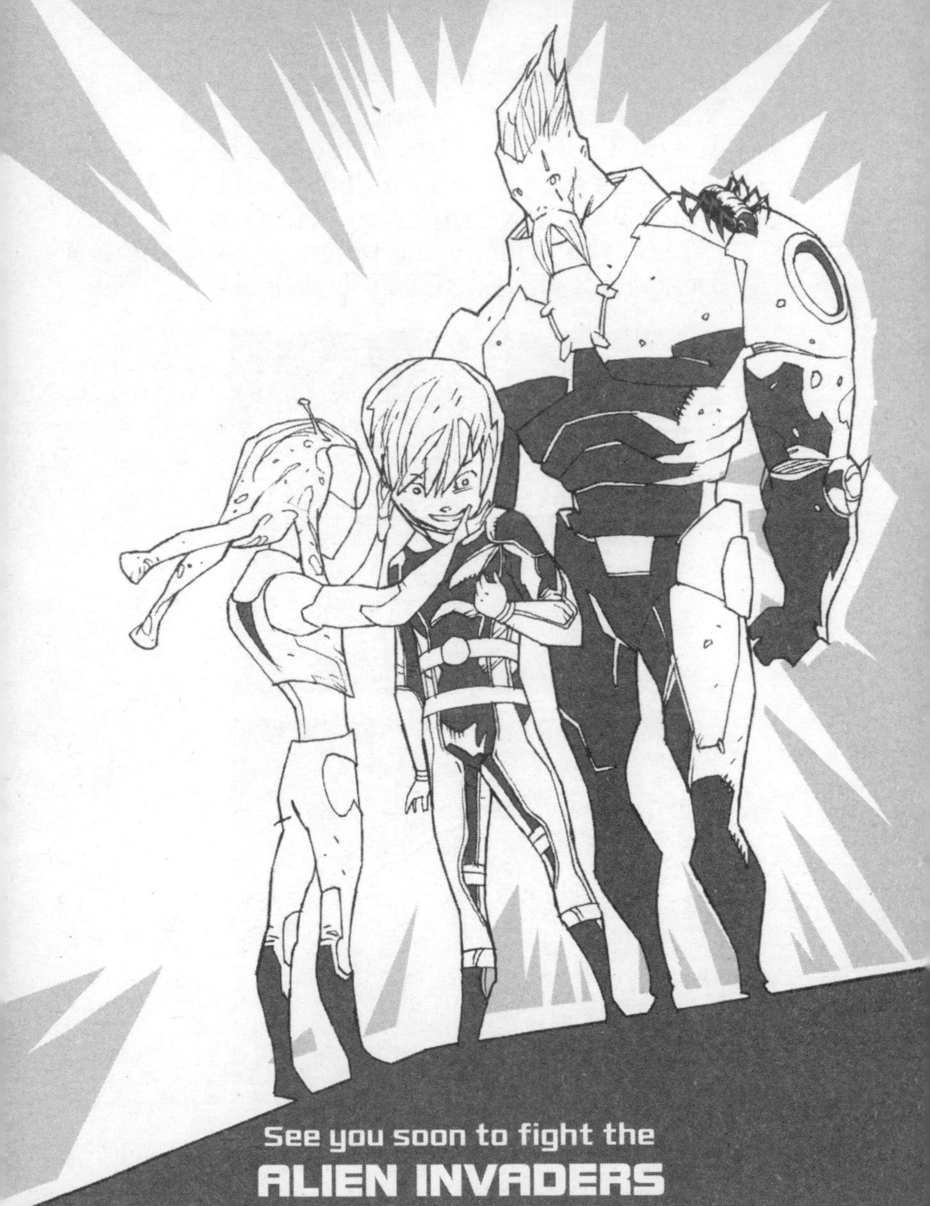

See you soon to fight the
ALIEN INVADERS
from THE WRECKING ZONE.
G-WATCH NEEDS YOU!